the Addams Family ™

GIRLFRIENDSTEIN

Published by The Trumpet Club
666 Fifth Avenue, New York, New York 10103

ISBN 0-440-84919-5

Produced by Parachute Press, Inc.
Printed in the United States of America
February 1993

1 3 5 7 9 10 8 6 4 2

CWO

The Addams Family

GIRLFRIENDSTEIN

by Kelli Finnegan

A TRUMPET CLUB ORIGINAL BOOK

One

A thick mist hung all around the Addams family mansion. The weather was cold and creepy. Vultures circled the house, flying in and out of the craggy trees, occasionally swooping down to pick at a dead rat. It was, to sum up, a perfect day. Just right for the weirdest family in Happydale Heights.

"Ah, Tish," Gomez Addams said to his wife, Morticia. "It wouldn't be Sunday without our back-yard brunches. A hearty meal, family togetherness," he sighed happily. He gazed around the tumbledown gazebo where they sat, then out at the crumbling mansion and the family cemetery. Who could ask for more? By gosh, he was one lucky guy!

Morticia Addams smiled and looked out past the barbed-wire bridge and the alligator swamp to the great lawn. "And just look at our two little dears playing so sweetly," she said.

Wednesday and Pugsley, the beloved Addams children, waved to their parents. The kids were playing a game called shell shock, which was a lot like croquet but with one big difference.

Pugsley replaced his croquet ball with a round black bomb. "I strike at thee, Sir Pugsley," said Wednesday. She tossed her long black braids and aimed her mallet. *Thwack!* She hit her ball with the mallet. It zipped through the wicket and smacked into Pugsley's bomb-ball with a big *booooomm!*

Pugsley went flying over the great lawn and the alligator swamp and came crashing down through the center of the breakfast table.

"Well, Pugsley, I see you've worked up an appetite!" said Morticia. She offered Pugsley a brownie from the dessert plate. But when she looked at the goodies more closely, she wrinkled her nose and set them back down. "Gomez, did you notice that the brownies aren't moving?"

"That's odd," said Gomez. "Better not eat them, Pugsley, my boy. They're not fresh!"

"It's not like Lurch to be so careless," Morticia said.

"Maybe there's an explanation," Gomez replied

as he pulled on the long rope beside the table. The sound of a gong shook the walls of the house.

Their ten-foot-tall butler, Lurch, instantly appeared at the table holding a silver tray full of snacks. "Cocktail wieners?" he groaned.

"Not now, old man. Just put them down any-where," Gomez answered. "By the way, Lurch, old boy, what's new with you lately? Spill your secrets!"

Lurch looked off into space and let go of the tray. It hit the floor with a *crash!*

Morticia was delighted. Lurch was being his normal self today, after all. "Lurch, dear, if some-thing were wrong, you'd tell us, wouldn't you?" she asked him.

Lurch let out an extra-loud and extra-painful moan. "Uhhhhhhhhhhhhhhhh!"

"He sounds fine to me," Gomez said.

"Uhhhhhhh," said Lurch again. He lowered his head and turned to go. He took one step and tripped over Pugsley's electric train. Teetering off-balance, he fell forward and made a perfect Lurch-shaped hole in the latticework wall of the gazebo. From the other side of the wall came a familiar groan. "Uuuhhhhhhhhhhhhh!"

Morticia and Gomez jumped up in alarm. This was a bit much, even for Lurch!

Uncle Fester, who had been practicing belly flops in the compost heap, heard the crash. He ran to the gazebo and there he found Lurch lying face down in the dirt.

"Lurch, old buddy, old pal, speak to me!" cried Uncle Fester. "Are you hurt? Any bones broken?" He paused and looked closely at the dirt near Lurch's face. "Are you going to eat that earthworm?"

Everyone waited for some sign of life from Lurch. Wednesday knew that something big was troubling her friend. "What's wrong, Lurch? Please tell us!"

From the ground came Lurch's deep, quiet voice. "No comment."

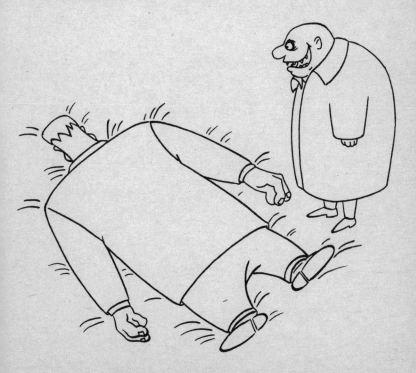

TWO

I t was clear that Lurch just wasn't himself. But he refused to tell anyone about what was bothering him.

"Uncle Fester, Mom, and Dad can't get Lurch to tell them anything," Wednesday told Pugsley. "He won't even answer *my* questions, no matter how sneaky they are. Lurch is in a really big, really bad mood, and we've got to find out why!"

"What can we do?" Pugsley asked. "Lurch was never much of a talker."

"I say we sneak into his room to search for clues," said Wednesday. "All agreed?"

Pugsley raised his right hand in salute and said, "Aye." Across the room, a beautiful wooden box

opened and a pale, bony hand came out—Pugsley's
pet hand, Thing. With his thumb and forefinger,
Thing made an "okay" sign.

"Thank you, Thing," Wednesday said.

"Thing always votes with me!" Pugsley said
proudly.

"So we're all agreed," said Wednesday. "Let's
go!"

She led the way up the narrow stairs to Lurch's
room. Pugsley crept along behind her, and Thing got
a free ride on Pugsley's head.

The door to Lurch's room was made for a giant.
Wednesday reached for the bottom handle, and
Thing sprang up to get the top knob. Pugsley leaned
his pudgy body against the door, and they all pushed
hard until it opened. Then they sneaked in and
shoved the door closed behind them.

"All right! Let's rummage!" said Pugsley. He ran
over to Lurch's dresser and opened the drawers,
throwing Lurch's white dress shirts everywhere.

Wednesday checked out the bedside table,
looked under the bed, and peeked into Lurch's closet.
When she saw the mess her brother had made, she
rushed over and grabbed him. "You're no help!" she
cried. She was about to tie him up when Thing
snapped his fingers to get their attention.

Thing pointed to the wastebasket in the corner
of Lurch's room. Sticking out of it was a huge shoe-

box. Wednesday and Pugsley ran over to look at it.

"Size 27, width QQQQ. That's Lurch's size," Pugsley said.

"Let's see if anything's inside." Wednesday pulled off the top and started poking around the box. "Oh! Personal stuff!" she cried.

"Any food?" Pugsley asked.

Wednesday ignored him. "Gosh," she said. "This box is full of love letters!"

Pugsley grabbed one of the letters and read it aloud. "Roses are red, violets are blue, sugar is sweet, uhhhhh!"

Wednesday nearly fainted. "That's beautiful—in a Lurch sort of way," she said. She reached into the box again and pulled out a picture of a gigantic glum-faced young woman. "Look at this!" she said. "This must be Lurch's girlfriend! She looks just like a girl Lurch. Gee, she's pretty."

Pugsley picked up another letter in the box. "Listen to this one! 'Dear Lurch, It is so sad when one monster feels more than another. I must go where I am wanted. Wishing you a rotten life. Uhhhhhhh!'"

Wednesday sadly shook her head. "Oh, no! Lurch's girlfriend dumped him! We've got to tell Mom and Dad." Wednesday forced Pugsley to put Lurch's shirts back where they belonged. Then she took the box and they headed downstairs.

They found their parents in the parlor and showed them the "Dear Lurch" letter.

"No wonder Lurch has been so sad," Morticia said. "Family, we need to come together to help poor heartbroken Lurch."

"We'll make him feel loved!" exclaimed Gomez. "A little torture to cheer him up, fun and games, you know, memories of better times." Gomez hugged his children.

"Let's bring down the rack and some of Lurch's other favorite instruments of torture from the attic to surprise him," Morticia suggested.

Lurch served dinner. After the dishes were thrown away and all the leftovers were wrestled into the refrigerator, they all went upstairs.

Gomez and Morticia led everyone up to the musty attic. Wednesday stopped along the way to pick some pretty cobwebs out of the nooks and crannies to make a necklace for her mother.

When the creaky attic door opened, Wednesday and Pugsley stared in amazement. They hadn't been in the attic in years. It was filled with treasures!

There were tons of amazing things—suits of Chinese armor, huge anchors, half a chiseled tombstone, coffins, a wrapped-up mummy, a stuffed polar bear. One corner was devoted to Uncle Fester's old inventions.

Gomez picked up a set of teeth with fangs in

them. "Granny's original choppers," he said fondly. Against the wall was an old black baby carriage with prison bars on it. "Ah, my old baby carriage," he added. "This place is full of charming memories."

Morticia opened a large trunk in the center of the room. "Look, little ghastlings, a picture of dear Uncle Fester before he shed his first head."

Gomez picked through a pile of old clothes and asked, "Don't we have that ol' noggin kicking around up here somewhere?"

Morticia dug deeper into the trunk and came out with a giant framed portrait—Lurch's baby picture. She passed the picture to the children. It showed an unsmiling baby Lurch in diapers, holding a silver tray with a pacifier on it.

"Great guns in August!" Gomez shouted from behind some old dinosaur bones. "Guess what I've found!"

"Uncle Fester's first head?" Pugsley asked hopefully.

Wednesday jumped up and down in excitement. "Does the third eye still blink?"

"No, something better! It's the one and only hiding horn! I thought it was lost. It sure brings back the memories." Gomez was beaming. "The hiding horn game was Lurch's favorite. Oh, the times we used to have! Fester has got to see this." He turned to his daughter and said, "Wednesday, dear, please ask your uncle Fester to come up and join us."

"My pleasure, Dad," Wednesday said quietly. She opened the attic door and shouted down the stairs, "Behold! A pile of ants!"

Fester dashed to the attic in seconds, carrying a bottle of ketchup and a spoon. He ran in circles around the kids trying to catch ant snacks. "Where? Where?" he asked eagerly.

Gomez held up the end of the giant hiding horn for Fester to see.

Fester gasped. "Do I dare believe my sore, bloodshot, itchy eyes?" he said. "It's the hiding horn! After all these years!"

"Dad?" asked Pugsley. "What's the big deal about some old horn?"

"Only the greatest game we ever played, son!" said Gomez. "Kind of a worldwide hide-and-seek. First we'd blow the horn as loud as we could."

"Hopefully passing out from the effort!" said Fester.

"At the sound of the horn we had a five-second head start on old Lurchy boy! We could hide *anywhere in the world,* and the poor guy would have until midnight to find us."

Morticia looked up from the pair of three-eyed reading glasses she was holding. "And he always did," she remembered fondly.

"That's right, Tish," Gomez sighed. "Forget the

rack—I don't think medieval torture is going to do the trick this time! Forget the baby pictures! The hiding horn is guaranteed to make Lurch lose those boo-hoo blues!"

Fester grinned. "A rematch! Us against Lurch. Just like the good old days!"

"Give me a hand, Fester," said Gomez, "and we'll take the horn downstairs. Just wait until Lurch hears the call of the hiding horn once more! He'll forget all about what's-her-name!"

Three

Lurch stood looking up at the living room ceiling. "Uhhhhh . . ." he sighed. He placed a cobweb in an empty corner, then smiled, but only for a brief moment.

Gomez and Fester walked in wearing mountain-climbing gear and carrying maps, flashlights, and backpacks. "Bad news for you, old friend," Gomez said with a jolly grin. "We found the hiding horn!"

Lurch gave Gomez a long-suffering look. "Uhhhhh . . ." he said, hanging his head.

"Ready for a bit of sport, Lurch, old boy?" Gomez asked. "For old times' sake?"

Lurch shrugged his huge shoulders with a "why me?" look on his face.

"We'll play a five-rounder," said Fester. "Gomez and I get five chances to hide—and *you* get five chances to find us. We're bound to win *at least* one round!"

Lurch just gave one extra-long groan and lumbered away toward the mousetraps in the den. It was nine o'clock and dinner was long over, so Lurch needed a snack to get him through the next few hours.

Fester and Gomez gathered the family around the hiding horn. *"Cara mia!* Wish us luck!" Gomez said to his wife.

Morticia kissed him on the forehead. "Good luck, darling," she said.

Pugsley shook hands with Uncle Fester and his father. "We know you can do it, Dad!" he said, beaming.

Wednesday hugged her father. "Break a leg, Dad."

Gomez put a loving hand on Wednesday's cheek and sighed, "I can only wish, my dear!" Then he said, "Ready, Fester?"

"Ready!" Fester took a deep breath and blew into the horn with all his might. The deep, hollow sound blasted through the mansion, and Gomez and Fester took off!

Four

Gomez and Fester ran upstairs and dived into the first closet they came to. It was pitch dark, and not a sound was to be heard. "We're off to a booming start, Fester," Gomez whispered.

Fester turned on a flashlight. "We've got him now!" he said, smiling broadly.

The brothers grinned confidently and looked around them. Then their mouths dropped open. Lurch was standing right behind them, wearing sunglasses. "Uhhhhhh," he said.

Gomez and Fester jumped out of the closet. They flew down the stairs and ran out the door.

"Come on," Gomez shouted, "jump in the car!"

They leaped into the family hearse, which was parked right in front of the house.

Gomez started driving. "Where are we going?" Fester asked as they sped down the driveway.

Suddenly Lurch popped up behind them in the back seat.

"Let's get out of here!" cried Fester.

"I can't believe he found us again," said Gomez. "Rats! This might not be as easy as I thought!"

Gomez and Fester jumped out of the moving hearse as it rolled through the massive front gate and began to run back toward the Addams mansion. Behind them, they heard the hearse crash into another car. A man screamed.

"Well, at least someone's having a good day," said Gomez.

"Hiding horn game, huh, Gomez?" whined Fester, panting heavily as he pushed himself to keep up. "We're total losers. We're worse at this game now than when we were kids!"

Gomez jogged along at a brisk pace. "Be a sport, old man. This game isn't about how good we are at hiding," Gomez said. "Our job is to cheer up Lurch!"

"But we can't cheer up Lurch if he finds us so easily," said Fester. "Lurch likes a challenge."

"Never fear, Fester dear! I know a place where even a crafty bloodhound like Lurch won't find us!"

Five

Gomez chuckled as he ran around the house and out onto the Addams airstrip, with Fester following close behind. They boarded the family plane. Gomez put on his old flying helmet, long silk scarf, and goggles. Then he revved up the engine, and they took off.

They flew over Happydale Heights, across the ocean, and far out into the Sahara Desert.

"Lurch is history," Gomez yelled above the roar of the engines. "I'm going in for a landing, so hold on, brother dear!"

Gomez landed the plane behind a sand dune, then he and Fester jumped out. To their surprise, they saw that they weren't alone. A short, hairy blob was sitting behind the dune in a beach chair, sunning itself.

"Cousin Itt!" cried Fester. "What in the world are you doing here?"

"Terwweeetzlblrb glt leeb," said Cousin Itt.

"You're here on vacation?" said Gomez. "That's nice. We're in the middle of a game of hiding horn. Care to join us?"

"Gweelopstrmp," said Cousin Itt.

"He'd love to!" said Gomez excitedly. "We're thrilled that you can join us."

It was high noon in Africa. The hot sun beat down on them. Gomez fell to his knees and wiped the sweat from his brow.

"We've got to find water," said Gomez. He and Fester and Cousin Itt began to crawl across the desert, looking for water.

"Fester," Gomez panted, "the vultures are starting to circle."

"Well, if you'd hold still for a second," Fester snapped, "one of them might just come closer and start pecking your head!"

Gomez sighed. "That would be marvelous—nothing like a good headache! Too bad we have to keep moving."

They crawled on. Suddenly Fester bumped into something. It was a large shoe—a *very* large shoe. Squinting against the glare of the sun, Fester slowly looked up. There was Lurch! Large as life.

"Uuhhhhh . . . lemonade?" Lurch asked, holding a tray with ice-cold glasses and a frosty pitcher of drinks.

"Aaahhhhhh!" screamed Gomez and Fester. They raced for the plane, dragging Cousin Itt along with them, and flew back home to Happydale Heights.

"So much for that," said Gomez. "If Lurch can find us in the Sahara Desert, then he can find us anywhere!"

It was already eleven o'clock at night by the time they got back to the house. Cousin Itt decided to drop out of the game and play with Wednesday and Pugsley instead.

Only one more hour—and two rounds—to go.

"Gomez, I've got an idea," said Fester. "To my lab, quick!"

In Fester's lab, Gomez watched while Fester mixed a brew of bright chemicals in two beakers.

"My latest invention," he said. "I think this will do the trick. Lurch can't find us if he can't see us!" He handed his brother a foaming beaker.

"To hiding!" said Gomez, raising his glass in a toast.

The brothers drank. Soon they felt a fizzing in their stomachs. Their faces turned blue. Then their eyes popped, and they disappeared! There was nothing left of them but their floating clothes.

"Now," Fester whispered, "all we have to do is take off our clothes and we're completely invisible. Lurch will never find us!"

Gomez took off his jacket. A large hand took it from him, folding it neatly.

"Thanks, Lurch," Gomez said.

"Uhhhhhh," said Lurch.

"No! No, no, no!" Fester groaned. Lurch had found them again.

The invisibility potion wore off as Gomez and Fester ran to hide in Fester's bedroom.

"No matter what we do, Lurch always finds us," said Gomez sadly.

"I tell you, Gomez, he's got eyes in the back of his head!" Fester said. "Or was that Cousin Slime Mold?"

"No, *he* had ears on his ankles," said Gomez, slumping down.

"That's right," Fester agreed.

"There's only one round left, and it's almost midnight." Gomez threw up his hands in surrender. "We might as well give up."

"Give up?" cried Fester. "Never! This calls for drastic measures." He pulled out a remote control. "My emergency hiding place. I was hoping it wouldn't come to this, but we're desperate."

Gomez pulled out his pocket watch. It was five

minutes to midnight. "Whatever it is, Fester, hurry up and do it," Gomez sighed. "We're running out of time."

Fester pushed the button and closed his eyes. They sat there for a long moment. Nothing happened.

Then *wham!* A hundred-ton weight dropped out of nowhere and smashed down on them, flattening them to the floor.

Just then Lurch wandered through the room and looked around. He saw the hundred-ton weight with two pairs of feet sticking out from under it. But he ignored them. He took another look around the room and left. Lurch thought he might as well let them win. After all, they were trying so hard. When he was gone, he wanted the Addamses to have fond memories of him.

Another minute passed, and the clock struck midnight.

Gomez and Fester pulled themselves out from under the weight, flat as pancakes.

"We did it! After all these years!" Gomez hugged his brother. "Fester, you're a genius! We've finally outwitted Lurch," he said happily. Then he put a hand to his aching back. "This is a moment to remember!"

Lurch was hiding just outside the room, listening. He peeked in on the happy brothers and smiled. Then he turned to leave . . . and bumped into

Wednesday and Pugsley. They had seen everything.

"Confess, Lurch," Wednesday whispered. "You knew they were under that weight all the time, didn't you?"

Lurch nodded. "Uhhhh."

Gomez and Fester came out of the room and saw Lurch and the children in the hallway.

"Great game of hiding horn, eh, Lurch?" said Gomez, totally unaware that Lurch had let them win.

Lurch didn't say a word.

"What's the matter, Lurch?" asked Wednesday. "Didn't the game cheer you up?"

Lurch shook his head and lumbered away.

"Poor Lurch," said Wednesday. "We've got to do something about his love life—and fast!"

Six

The next morning Pugsley and Wednesday woke up to bluebirds chirping a happy tune, a sky filled with fluffy clouds, and the sun shining for all to see. They knew it was going to be a really bad day!

Wednesday and Pugsley were chasing their breakfast through the house when they suddenly stopped short. They saw something horrible—the most terrible sight they'd ever seen in their lives.

It was Lurch, carrying a huge suitcase in each hand. He was headed for the door. He was leaving!

"Noooooo!" Wednesday screamed.

Gomez, Morticia, Fester, Thing, and Cousin Itt came running when they heard the scream. Everyone

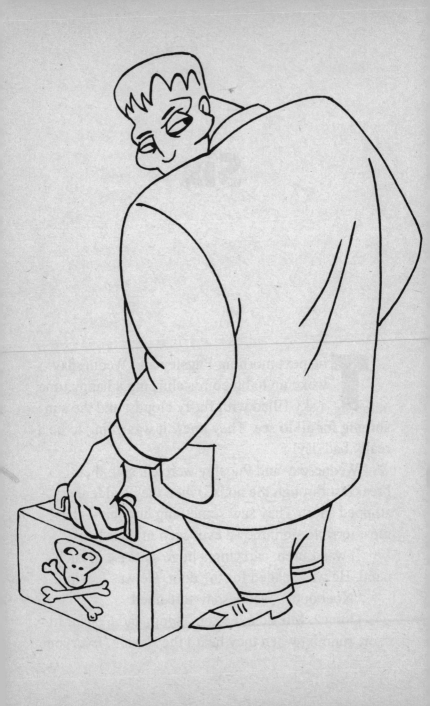

grabbed onto Lurch's coattail, trying to hold him back. But Lurch simply dragged the family along with him toward the door.

Thing broke away and gave a sharp tug on the hall rug. Lurch flew up, then landed on his flat head. One by one, Gomez, Morticia, Fester, Wednesday, Pugsley, and Cousin Itt landed on top of their devoted servant.

"Thank you, Thing," said Morticia, straightening her tight spidery gown and smoothing her long black hair.

Thing made the okay sign, then shook his finger at Lurch, scolding him.

"Thing's right, Lurch," Pugsley said. "You should be ashamed, trying to sneak away like that!"

"This was a great early-morning game, big fellah, but what gives?" asked Gomez.

Lurch rolled his eyes and moaned so loudly it broke a few windows in the room. "Uuhhh . . . noooooo."

Gomez put his arms around Lurch and said, "Lurch, old man, we know what's bothering you. It's that girl, isn't it?"

Lurch nodded sadly.

"But Lurch, she's just a girl," Gomez said. "And we're family! Besides, where else would you go, and how will leaving help? And as the saying goes, there are plenty of other sharks in the sea."

Lurch looked wistfully at his suitcases, then slowly dragged them back to his room. Everyone watched him with concern.

Wednesday tugged at Fester's sleeve. "We have a crisis on our hands, Uncle Fester! Lurch really needs our help!"

Fester was munching on some lint from the lining of his nightcap. "What do you want me to do? I'm no good at this love business. All I know how to do is invent things."

Gomez's eyes lit up. "Fester! Eureka! That's it!"

"What's it?" Fester asked.

"I get it, Dad!" said Wednesday. "Uncle Fester can invent a new girlfriend for Lurch!"

Fester cocked his head and grinned. "You mean, build a girl? I don't know. . ."

Morticia took Fester's arm. "Please, Fester darling," she purred. "For Lurch."

Fester took off his nightcap and rubbed his shiny bald head. "Well, when you put it that way. . . . Okay, I'll try it! One made-to-order girlfriend coming up!" Fester paused. "Maybe," he said, and he sped off to his lab.

Morticia smiled and folded her arms. "Isn't this lovely? Lurch will be so surprised."

Seven

Uncle Fester puttered around in the lab, trying to figure out what to do. He had never made a "girlfriend" before.

"This is going to take some thought," he mumbled to himself. He waited, but no thoughts came to him.

"Maybe I need some refreshment first," he said.

He grabbed a beaker from a burner and drank its contents. "Ah, a nice cup of lice tea!" he said. "Just the thing for a little pick-me-up!"

He settled into his favorite chair and prepared to be brilliant. He waited and waited, but nothing happened.

"Maybe I'll do a few exercises to get the ol'

brain boiling," he said to his favorite spider, Buggsy.

Fester sat up straight and cracked his fingers, right hand, then left hand. "Music to my ears!" he said with a chuckle.

"Head exercises next, Buggsy, my buddy. First the noggin goes round and round," he said as he spun his head completely around, a full 360 degrees, twice in a row.

"Now that it's unscrewed," he said, twisting his head with his hands and pulling it off his shoulders, "the noggin goes up and down." He lifted his head up high over his shoulders, then brought it down to his feet.

"There! I feel much better now," he said as he screwed his head back on and went to work.

Eight

Meanwhile, Wednesday and Pugsley were upstairs trying to get Lurch ready to meet his new girlfriend.

"I think you could use a little sprucing up, Lurch," said Wednesday. She picked up a comb, and Lurch groaned.

"Relax, Lurch!" said Wednesday. "Your hair will soon be nice and ratty." She tried to pull the comb through Lurch's steely hair, but with the very first stroke all the teeth snapped off.

"Your hair broke another comb, Lurch," said Wednesday. She sighed and added, "I wish I had hair like yours."

Thing appeared with a brand-new comb.

"Thank you, Thing," Wednesday said, turning back to Lurch. "We want you to look your worst—uh, just in case you happen to meet someone—uh, you know, just in case."

Pugsley was picking lint from Lurch's coat and eating it. "Whoever she is, I hope she's nicer than your last girlfriend!"

Lurch turned even paler than usual and gave out a sad moan. Then he stood up and thumped out of the room.

"Good going, fish brain," Wednesday snapped at her brother. "Now Lurch is more depressed than ever. And you almost gave away the surprise!"

"It just slipped out," said Pugsley apologetically.

"Lurch is a great catch," Wednesday said. "He's really cute, he's really nice, and he can always carry you if you get tired. His problem is that he's not good at talking. He doesn't know how to share his feelings. I bet his girlfriend had no idea how much he liked her."

Just then Uncle Fester wandered by, absent-mindedly scratching his head.

"Uncle Fester!" called Wednesday. "How's it going down there?"

"Yeah!" said Pugsley. "When do we get to see the new girlfriend?"

"Chill out, kids!" said Fester. "These things take time."

"But Lurch is getting desperate!" said Wednesday.

"He'll just have to wait," said Fester. "I can't create a girlfriend out of thin air, you know!"

Nine

Fester searched through the house for the things he needed to make Lurch's new girlfriend.

"Let's see," said Fester, pacing back and forth. "What do I need to make a body? Wood? Metal?"

Fester wasn't sure what he should use to make the girlfriend. "I think I'll just go outside and see what I can dig up," he said.

He went outside and started across the great lawn toward the family cemetery. Suddenly the earth began to quiver and quake. Fester stopped and looked around.

Stomp, Stomp, Stomp. A big dinosaur lumbered out of the alligator swamp. He craned his long neck and gave Fester a big wet sloppy dinosaur kiss.

"Leroy!" Fester cried happily, patting the reptile on the head. Leroy was Pugsley's pet dinosaur.

Leroy bent his head to the ground and picked up a stick in his mouth. Then he dropped it at Fester's feet.

"Oh, so you want to play fetch, do you, boy?" said Fester. "Okay. I guess I've got time for a short game."

Fester picked up the stick and tossed it into the alligator swamp.

"Fetch, Leroy!" he called.

Leroy took off after the stick. He jumped into the alligator swamp, but the stick had sunk to the murky bottom. Leroy couldn't find it.

Leroy climbed out of the swamp, whining.

"Aw," said Fester. "You lost your stick. Don't be sad, old pal. We can still play fetch. Just pick up another stick."

Leroy wagged his big scaly tail. He stomped over to the edge of the graveyard, started digging a big hole, and picked up a skeleton in his mouth. He carried it over to Fester and dropped it—*crash!*—right on top of him.

"Ouch," Fester whimpered. The skeleton had broken up into a pile of bones. Then a light bulb went off in Fester's head. Bones! *That's* what he could use to make the girlfriend. It was a start, in

46

any event. He would take it from there.

"Good dino," he said weakly to Leroy. "That's enough fetch for now. Go lie down somewhere in the next county."

He picked up the bones and limped back to his lab. Then he began to work furiously.

Suddenly a big explosion shook the house. Wednesday and Pugsley could hear their uncle laughing like a maniac.

"It's almost done! At last! I can't believe it!" Fester's voice came up through a vent in the floor and rang through the house.

"Cool!" said Pugsley.

Wednesday grabbed a handful of her brother's hair and dragged him toward the stairs. "Let's get down to the lab," she said. "I can't wait to see Lurch's new girlfriend!"

Ten

Wednesday and Pugsley crept down to Fester's lab. It was dark down there, except for the weird glow coming from Fester's machines. Bright blue neon arcs flew across the room, lighting something under a sheet on a slab table. Fester pulled levers and cackled maniacally. Electrical bolts shot through the slab and a tiny bell rang. Fester danced merrily around the table.

Pugsley couldn't stand the suspense any longer. "Uncle Fester!" he shouted, pointing to the figure that lay on the slab table. "Is that Lurch's new girlfriend?"

"No, silly!" Fester giggled and pulled the sheet off the slab. "It's my monkey-hair hoagie!"

On the table was a long hero sandwich. Fester picked it up and took a bite. "Delicious! Of course, they get a little gummy when you microwave them."

Wednesday put her hands on her hips and glared at her uncle. "Where's Lurch's girlfriend, Uncle Fester?" she demanded. "Haven't you started working on her yet?"

"Oh, she's been done for hours," Fester replied, gesturing over his shoulder with his thumb. "She's in the closet behind me."

Wednesday and Pugsley went to the closet and opened the door. Inside was a female robot. "What's her name?" Pugsley asked.

"Mary Lou!" Fester answered, beaming.

Mary Lou had thick brown hair and a lumpy, barely human-looking face. Her body was made of bones and metal, with a filing drawer where her stomach would be. Instead of legs she moved around on one wheel.

"She's hideous, Uncle Fester! A job well done!" said Wednesday.

"How does she work?" asked Pugsley.

"Simple!" Fester said. He opened Mary Lou's filing drawer and pulled something out. "Behold, the remote control for my handy Dial-a-Brain. This lets Lurch pick the personality of his choice! Watch!" He pushed a button on the remote control.

With a metallic arm, Mary Lou pulled a gavel

from her drawer and pounded the table. "I have twenty . . . . Do I hear twenty-five? . . . Twenty-five . . . twenty-five . . . looking for twenty-five . . . . Twenty-five in the corner!"

"I don't think Lurch wants an auctioneer girlfriend, Uncle Fester," Wednesday said.

Disappointed, Fester pushed another button. "Let's try this one."

The robot's brown hairstyle magically changed into a ponytail. She looked around excitedly and said, "So, like, where is this big blue half-dead slab of manstuff?"

Wednesday nodded. "That's better," she said. Then she pointed to the door at the top of the stairs. "He's in there!" she told the robot.

Mary Lou whizzed through the door. "Ohmigosh! I am totally beside myself with excitement!" she exclaimed.

Meanwhile, Gomez and Morticia were preparing Lurch for the big moment. "Lurch, old man, we have a surprise for you," said Gomez. He handed Lurch a bouquet of roses. Lurch just stood there looking at the flowers with distaste.

"No, no, Gomez," said Morticia. "That bouquet won't do. Lurch, dear, let me get you some lovely dead flowers. Those are so ugly!" She chopped the heads off the roses and added some rotting flowers and dead branches to the bouquet. "There, that's

51

so much better!" Simply irresistible!

"Uhhhhhhh . . . thank you," Lurch said, clutching the dried stalks.

Then Mary Lou came wheeling around the corner. Fester, Wednesday, and Pugsley followed close behind. Mary Lou stopped in her tracks when she saw Lurch.

"Oh, my," she said. "What a corpselike hunk of man!"

Lurch looked startled. He turned to Gomez, then to Morticia. They smiled to encourage him.

"Go on, Lurch," said Gomez. "Talk to her."

"Aren't you, like, Lurch, the butler?" Mary Lou asked breathlessly.

"It depends," Lurch said cautiously.

Mary Lou leaned in closer, fluttering her eyelashes. "Don't you, like, play the pipe organ and sweep?" she asked.

Lurch backed away with a scowl. "Uuhhhhhhh," he groaned, not at all pleased!

"Ohhhhh!" The robot quivered with joy. "What a man! I could just die!"

"That's the spirit!" said Gomez.

Wednesday turned to Fester and said, "You'd better try another personality, Uncle Fester."

"Okay. Here's one Lurch is guaranteed to like!" Fester pushed a green button on the control box.

Mary Lou suddenly backed away from Lurch

with a *VROOM,* her one wheel screeching loudly. She sped around the room like a racecar, leaving a trail of exhaust behind her.

Lurch shook his head. He had a pained look on his face.

"Hmmph. I thought all men loved a nice car!" Fester said. "Let's try this." He pushed another button on the control box.

Mary Lou's hair began to grow longer and longer until it popped out in a big flip. With a mouthful of chewing gum she said, "My name's Mary Lou, sugar! Pleased to meetcha!" She held out her hand to Lurch.

Lurch tried to move away, but she grabbed his arm. "Come on, Lurchy. Let's go pick out his-and-hers matching gravestones. We're getting married!"

Lurch turned three shades of green and pulled his arm away. "Married, uhhh!" he gasped.

"We'll invite my whole family!" Mary Lou rattled on. "My mother, my father, my second cousin twice removed, my third cousin who moved twice . . . ." She counted each one on her fingers.

"Uh-uh!" Lurch shook his head in a definite *no*.

"And they'll move in with us and you can wait on them hand and foot . . ." Mary Lou screeched, holding Lurch tightly. "When you're not waiting on me, that is!"

Lurch took off so fast that Mary Lou was left

clutching his empty sleeve. "Hey, where'd ya go?" she said, and wheeled off to look for him.

"Isn't that sweet, dear?" Morticia said to her husband. "Lurch is playing hard to get."

Eleven

Thing was sitting in his open box on top of the dining room table when Mary Lou rolled around the corner. "Have you seen my Lurchy?" she asked.

Thing waved, signaling "no," and Mary Lou left the room.

"Thank you, Thing," Lurch growled, coming out from behind the dining room curtains.

Almost at once Mary Lou came back. "Oh, there you are, Lurchy-poo!" She carried a huge suitcase, which she put down with a thud beside Thing's box. "I packed everything you'll need for our honeymoon!" she said.

"Uhhhhhhhhhh!" Lurch groaned, defeated.

"I don't think Lurch likes Mary Lou," said Pugsley. Wednesday was holding him upside down over a tank filled with snapping alligators. Pugsley wriggled with delight.

"I know," Wednesday said sadly. "Uncle Fester's invention just isn't working out for Lurch."

Suddenly, the funeral-dirge doorbell rang. Wednesday ran to get it.

The entire family gathered around the doorway to see who it was.

There stood a gigantic Lurch-size woman. Wednesday recognized her from her photograph. It was Lurch's old girlfriend.

"Oh!" Wednesday said, smiling a big smile. "I was hoping you'd come back!"

Lurch entered the room and stared at the doorway in shock. "You're here?" he whispered.

The family stared at the big mystery woman and then at Lurch.

Wednesday invited the woman in. Then she turned to Lurch to explain. "I wrote to her, Lurch," said Wednesday. "I hope you don't mind. I told her you really care, but you just have a tiny problem expressing yourself!" Wednesday folded her arms over her chest, pleased that her plan had worked.

Lurch went to his ex-girlfriend and took her large hands in his. "Uhhhhhhh," he growled, and gave her a great big smile.

"Now, that's what I call an expression of love!" Gomez said, sweeping Morticia up in his arms and bending her backward.

Lurch patted Wednesday on the head. "Thank you, Wednesday," he groaned.

Then Mary Lou wheeled into the room with her bags packed, ready to leave forever. "Good-bye," she said to the Addamses. "I know when I'm not wanted." She started toward the door.

Just then Cousin Itt breezed into the room.

"Cousin Itt!" cried Gomez. "Join the party!"

"Yibbeeeerr, zeeezyssss blllottt!" Cousin Itt gibbered through his thick mass of hair. He nodded at Mary Lou.

"You like her, eh?" Gomez said, beaming. He leaned over to nudge the giant hair ball. "Go for it, Itt! You crafty devil!"

"Oh, Mary Lou!" Morticia called. "I don't believe you've met Cousin Itt."

Mary Lou turned around. She took one look at Cousin Itt and gasped. *"Caramba!* You're the hairiest heartthrob I've seen in a long time!"

"Yibbbberity, yayayahhhhhhaaaaa!" said Cousin Itt. He ran to her and gave her a furry hug. It was love at first sight!

"Yuck," said Pugsley. "All this lovey-dovey stuff is too much for me. Let's go play, Wednesday."

The children went over to the buzz saw at the other side of the room. "Wait for me, kids!" said Fester, following them.

Then Cousin Itt turned to Lurch and said, "Heeehwhahhah blzzzerri yyypebiityly."

"Isn't that sweet?" Morticia smiled. "Cousin Itt wants to double-date with Lurch and his girlfriend."

Gomez grinned, shaking his head. "Ahhhh! Just think how much fun two lumbering hulks, a robot, and a ball of hair can have together!" he said.

Morticia whispered into Gomez's ear, "We could get Fester to baby-sit and make it a triple date."

"Cara mia, you're a genius!" Gomez yelled. "What do you say, Fester? Are you free to baby-sit?"

Fester was tied to a log on a sawmill conveyor

belt. "You two snuggle-grubs go ahead!" he said, removing the gag from his mouth. "We're having fun! Right, kids?"

"Right, Uncle Fester!" Pugsley and Wednesday answered together.

Wednesday shoved the gag back into Fester's mouth, then Pugsley threw the lever, and the saw blade roared to life.

"We'll be fine!" Fester mumbled.

Wednesday guided her uncle toward the spinning blade. "Don't worry about us," she said to her parents. "We'll eat our steamed earthworms and go to bed early. We promise."

"Well, then, it's all set," said Gomez. He took Morticia's arm and added, "Shall we?"

The three couples left, heading toward the waiting car, a great big convertible hearse. Pugsley and Wednesday waved good-bye.

"After you," Lurch said, helping his girlfriend into the seat.

"Bbbbetllllliyyyyth," said Cousin Itt.

"How thoughtful!" Morticia said. "Itt has offered to drive so that Lurch can enjoy his night off!"

"But Cousin Itt is too short to see over the steering wheel," said Gomez. "He might drive off a cliff!"

Morticia smiled seductively. "Oh, darling,

wouldn't that be grand!" she said, hugging him.

"What a romantic night!" Gomez said.

"Bye-bye! Have fun, everybody!" Wednesday called.

"Don't forget to oil Mary Lou after dinner!" Fester mumbled through his gag.

Pugsley, Wednesday, and Uncle Fester resumed their game of buzz saw ride, and the night was filled with Uncle Fester's screams of delight.

"A perfect end to a perfect day!" Fester yelled above the roar.

Other Books about
The Addams Family™

FESTER'S UNBELIEVABLE
UNDERWEAR

IS COUSIN MUMBLES
HERE TO STAY?